CIRCLE

by

Mac Barnett

&

Jon Klassen

CANDLEWICK PRESS

This is Circle.

This is Circle's waterfall.

One day, Circle and Square and Triangle
played a game near her waterfall.
"Here are the rules," Circle said.
"I will close my eyes and count to ten.
You must hide somewhere.
When I open my eyes, I will try to find you."
Square said, "OK."
Triangle said, "Neat!"

"There is one more rule," said Circle.
"No hiding behind the waterfall."
 Square said, "OK."
 Triangle said, "Why not?"
"Because," said Circle. "It is dark back there."
 Square said, "OK."
 Triangle said, "I am not afraid of the dark!"

Circle closed her eyes and counted to ten.
"Ready or not," said Circle, "here I come!"

When she opened her eyes,
Square was just standing there.
He pointed and said,
"Triangle went behind the waterfall."

Circle sighed. "I will go find him."

"Circle," said Square, "you are very brave."

"I know," Circle said.

And she slipped behind the waterfall.

It was quiet on the other side of the waterfall.

Circle called out, "Triangle! Triangle! Where are you?"

There was no answer.

Farther inside, there was not much light.
"Triangle! Triangle! Where are you!"

There was no answer. She went even farther

until it was all dark.

"Triangle!" said Circle. "There you are!
Why do you always break all the rules?"
There was no answer.

"Why do you always spoil our fun?"

There was no answer.

"Why are you such a bad friend?"

There was no answer.

"I'm sorry," said Circle.
"I should not have said that.
You are a good friend.
You just made us worried.
We love you, Triangle."

"Thanks!" Triangle said from behind her. Circle turned around and said, "Triangle?"

"Yes!" said Triangle. "I am sure glad to see you and Square!"

Circle said, "Square is outside.

This is not Square. I thought it was you."

"No," said Triangle, "that is not me."

"No," said Circle.

"Oh," said Triangle.

Circle turned back and faced the shape in the dark.
"Who are you?" she asked.

There was no answer.

"AAAH!" said Triangle.

Triangle and Circle ran very fast, back through the dark.

Back through where there was not much light.

Back through the waterfall, back to the outside.

Square was waiting there for them.

They told him what had happened.

"Well," Square said, "I am glad I stayed here!"

Triangle said, "Now I am afraid of the dark!"

Circle looked back at the waterfall falling.

"You know," she said, "that shape in the dark might

not have been bad. It might have been a good shape.

We just could not see it."

Circle closed her eyes.
"I wonder," Circle said. "What kind of shape was it?"

Then they all closed their eyes,

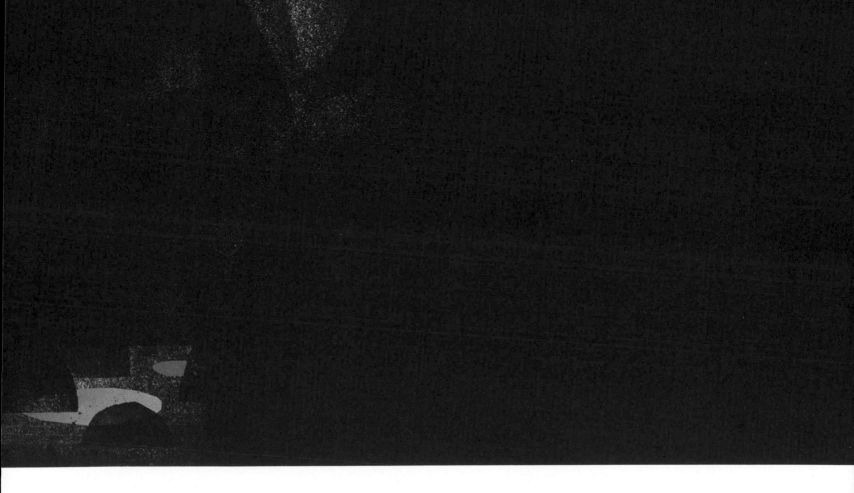

and they each pictured a shape.

If you close your eyes, what shape do you picture?

To the Villalongs:
Dan, Katherine, Elsa, Margot, and Helena

M. B.

For Ann Stott, with thanks for all you do

J. K.

MAC BARNETT & JON KLASSEN
have made six books together: *The Wolf, the Duck, and the Mouse,* which won an E. B. White Read Aloud Award and was an ALA Notable Children's Book and a *New York Times Book Review* Notable Children's Book of the Year; *Sam and Dave Dig a Hole,* which won a Caldecott Honor and an E. B. White Read Aloud Award; *Extra Yarn,* which won a Caldecott Honor, an E. B. White Read Aloud Award, and a *Boston Globe–Horn Book* Award; *Triangle; Square;* and *Circle,* which is the book you are reading right now. They both live in California, but in different cities. Jon's Canadian; Mac's not.

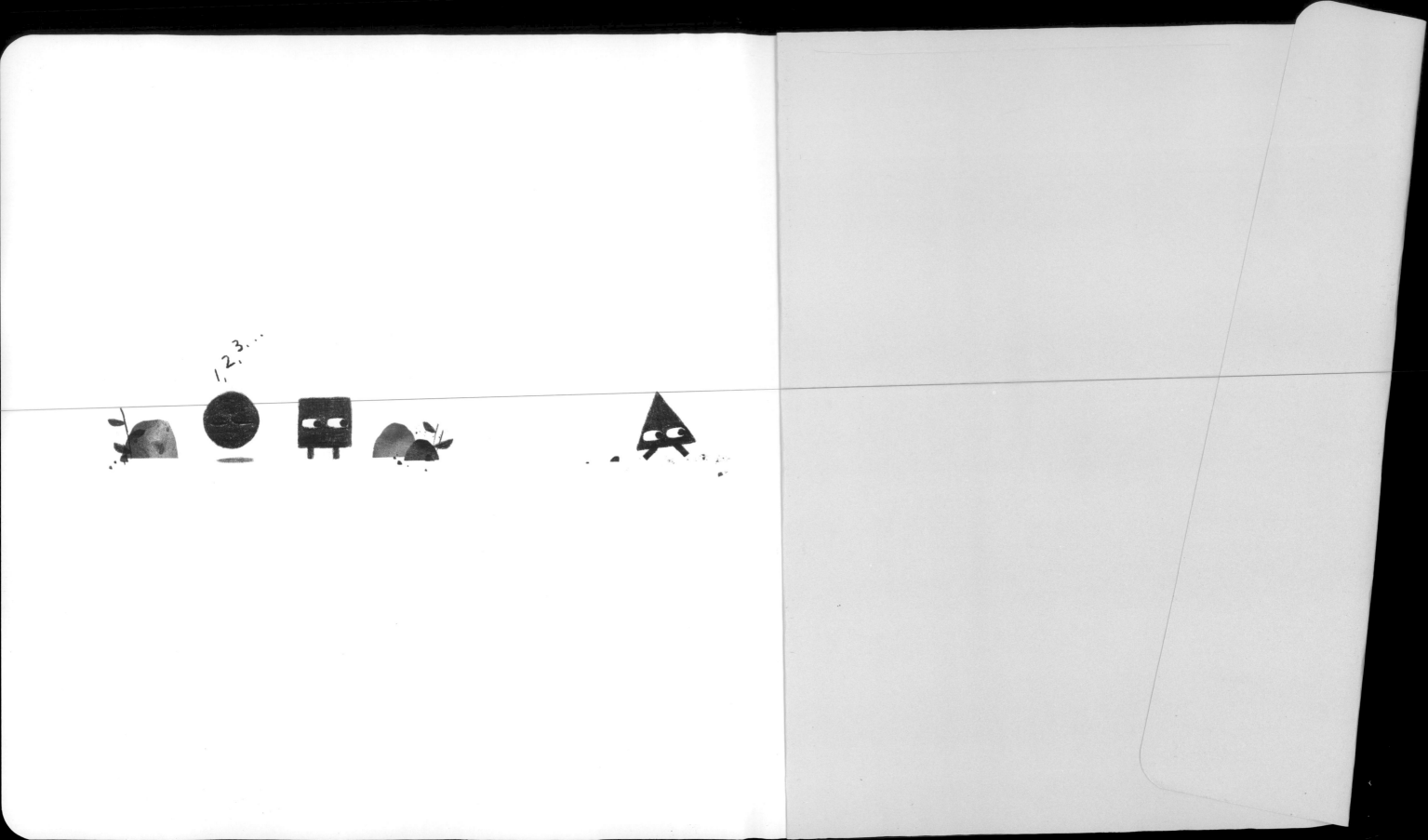

MAC BARNETT & JON KLASSEN
have made six books together: *The Wolf, the Duck, and the Mouse,* which won an E. B. White Read Aloud Award and was an ALA Notable Children's Book and a *New York Times Book Review* Notable Children's Book of the Year; *Sam and Dave Dig a Hole,* which won a Caldecott Honor and an E. B. White Read Aloud Award; *Extra Yarn,* which won a Caldecott Honor, an E. B. White Read Aloud Award, and a *Boston Globe–Horn Book* Award; *Triangle; Square;* and *Circle,* which is the book you are reading right now. They both live in California, but in different cities. Jon's Canadian; Mac's not.